OH, H
I DIDN'T
THI
*EDITOR'
BY ANYO
AND I'M
DOUG HOLGATE. I DO
THE RAD DRAWINGS AND
MAKE THE CHARACTERS
LOOK GOOD.
WE WANT
TO WELCOME YOU
TO THE NEWEST BOOK IN THE
LAST KIDS ON EARTH SERIES.
THIS ONE'S A BIT DIFFERENT,
BECAUSE...
!?
DUDES, WHAT
ARE YOU DOING IN
OUR BOOK?

WHAT GIVES?
EXCUSE ME, BUT WE ARE SUPPOSED TO BE THE STARS HERE.
JACK, THE ONLY REASON WHY YOU'RE THE MAIN CHARACTER IS BECAUSE I WROTE YOU.
AND I DREW YOU!

DON'T CARE. THIS IS **OUR** STORY. NOW SCRAM!

BUT I HAVE SO MANY GOOD IDEAS FOR WHAT'S GOING TO HAPPEN IN THIS BOOK!
YEAH, WELL, WE'RE KIND OF IN CHARGE NOW, SO BYEEEE.
I USED TO BE IN CHARGE HERE. HOW CAN IT BE THAT MY CREATIONS HAVE TAKEN ON A LIFE OF THEIR OWN?!
HELP US!
SOB!
YOU TWO REALLY NEED TO CALM DOWN.
OK, READERS. GO HAVE FUN WITH THE BOOK, PEACE OUT, BYE!
AIEEEEE!

MAX BRALLIER

& DOUGLAS HOLGATE

present:

THE LAST KIDS ON EARTH

SURVIVAL GUIDE

First published in the United States of America by Viking,
an imprint of Penguin Random House LLC, 2019

This edition published in 2023 by Farshore

An imprint of HarperCollins*Publishers*
1 London Bridge Street, London SE1 9GF

farshore.co.uk

HarperCollins*Publishers*
Macken House, 39/40 Mayor Street Upper,
Dublin, 1, D01 C9W8

ISBN 978 0 00 863817 7
Printed and bound in the UK using 100% renewable electricity at CPI Group (UK) Ltd
1

A CIP catalogueue record for this title is available from the British Library

Boring publishing stuff!

Flee!

Run away!

To Alyse, the best.

Welcome to the world of . . .

THE LAST KIDS ON EARTH

THIS BOOK BELONGS TO:

____

(Affix signature here for non-binding legal purposes)

A great book always seems to get messed up . . . Y'know — the book gets mashed in your backpack or Dirk sits on it or Rover slobbers on it or you get pizza grease on the pages.

Well, this is a GREAT BOOK — so let's mess it up RIGHT NOW!

Drool on this page and try to hit the bullseye — for real!

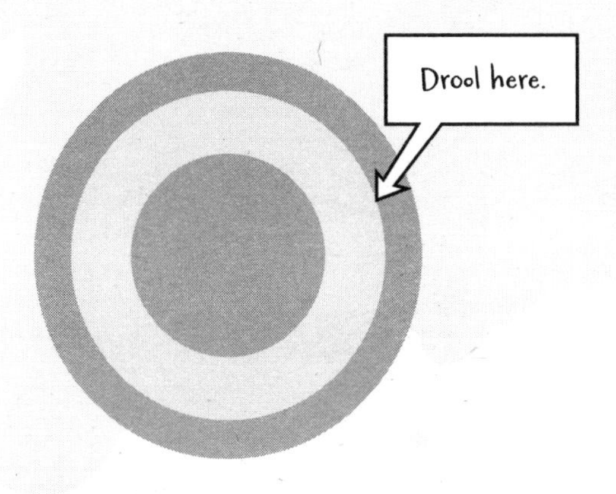

Good! This book's "mess up" is out of the way. Onward — time to do this thing!

MEET THE HEROES!

JACK! JUNE! QUINT! DIRK!
WITTY BANTER! GOOD TIMES!

The original title for the series was The Tree House at the End of the World.

Spear – for monster poking and zombie whacking.
QUINT BAKER
DIRK SAVAGE
5 o'clock shadow, even though he's only my age.
Jaw. Not to be messed with.
Newest gadget or experiment. Stand back!
Pocket watch for keeping track of time in style.
Boxing wraps. For punching things. (Always punching things.)
STRONG!
Steel-toed boots.
Wears a lab coat as a jacket when he wants to feel extra geeky.
Non-athlete's foot.

NOW YOU'RE THE HERO!

What if *you* were one of the last kids on earth? Draw yourself. Or tape in a selfie. Add your own arrows and labels!

- Harpoon with zip line. For escaping UP!
- Air-conditioned underwear. For cool comfort in the heat of battle.
- Rearview mirror. No more being snuck up on by giant monsters or annoying siblings.

Cut this page out and hang it on your door!

BRB
I'm out surviving the monster apocalypse!

BEST BUDDY QUIZ!

How close are you and your best friend, really? Take this quiz and find out! Circle one answer (A, B, C, or D) per question.

1. Your best friend has a tick stuck to his/her rear end. Do you remove it?

Ⓐ Yep. Will use a Quint-Inspired Automatic Distant Turbo-Charged Tick Remover.

Ⓑ Yes. Of course! (I think.)

Ⓒ No. Not even in the dark while wearing gloves.

Ⓓ Nope. Time for a new best friend.

2. Your buddy's breath stinks like hot garbage! What do you do?

Ⓐ Have a heart-to-heart talk. ('Cause it will **not** be a face-to-face talk.)

Ⓑ Come up with some crazy-complex Jack-inspired plan to save the day – or at least save your sense of smell.

Ⓒ Buy a gas mask.

Ⓓ Peace out! Time to get a new buddy!

3. It's the monster apocalypse! How far will you go to reunite with your buddy?

Ⓐ I will battle to the ends of this earth until we are together again!

Ⓑ I'll try – but not, like, **extra** hard.

Ⓒ I'll give my buddy a cool sword and then – bye! On your own!

Ⓓ Ehh, my pal can handle anything. I'm not worried. We don't need to hang out again. Ever.

4. Do you each know a pretty awful secret about each other?

Ⓐ And it doesn't matter? Yes!

Ⓑ Like I'd really tell you that!

Ⓒ What's it worth to you?

5. Got a secret handshake?

Ⓐ Yes. But neither of us can remember it.

Ⓑ Working on it!

Ⓒ No. Tried once. Decided never to do it again after the broken fingers and bloody noses.

6. You're accidentally handcuffed to your best friend? Is that an issue?

Ⓐ No. Until my best friend needs to use the toilet.

Ⓑ Maybe. Is this that friend with the bad breath?

Ⓒ Yes! Our friendship is as much about not being together as it is about being together.

7. You and your best friend pull off a heroic save-the-world mission. BUT! You're both captured and sent into eternal orbit. Who gets to ride shotgun in the spaceship?

Ⓐ We share shotgun. It's tight – but we get to ride **together**!

Ⓑ My best friend.

Ⓒ Me!

Ⓓ The weird alien hitchhiker we picked up.

8. Do you know your best bud's phone number by heart?

Ⓐ Together, my best friend and I have chosen to communicate ONLY via Morse code in-game chat.

Ⓑ Yes.

Ⓒ I think it has a 7 in it. . . And maybe a 19?

Ⓓ Bananas!

9. When you grow up, what will you name after your best friend?

Ⓐ Pet.

Ⓑ Car.

Ⓒ Lucky socks.

Ⓓ Dirty socks.

10. Your best bud turns out to be a nose picker.

Ⓐ That makes two of us (darn it).

Ⓑ Will recommend professional help.

Ⓒ It's over!

SCORING

Give yourself 5 points for every (A) answer, 4 points for every (B), 3 for every (C), and 1 for every (D).

______ (A) × 5 = ______

______ (B) × 4 = ______

______ (C) × 3 = ______

______ (D) × 1 = ______

TOTAL ______

Total points:

40–50: Best friends forever. Nothing can tear you two apart!

20–39: Good friends. You're there for each other most of the time. But honestly, not Hall of Famers.

0–19: Um . . . it might be time to find a new best buddy.

Map of Wakefield
This is where the action goes down!
Home Depot
Town forest
Fire station
CVS
Town park (now thick with Vine-Thingies)
Quint's house
The Old Box Factory (known Dozer lair)
The docks (sea monsters?!)
Parker Middle School

Christmas Tree Farm.
Atlantic Supermarket
Train tracks (home of the Tentacle Demon)
Town Square (home of our tree house, Joe's Pizza, and good-dude monsters!)
Old south graveyard
Big Al's Junk Palace (zombie cluster)
Historic Wakefield District
Town Library
ABC Movie Theatre

Your Own Post-Apocalyptic Playground!

Draw a map of your neighbourhood – then add monsters! Or create a town or city from scratch, using just your imagination!

COSTUME CHANGE!

Throughout the series, Jack and his buddies wear a bunch of different outfits. Dream up your own radical warrior wardrobe by tracing and drawing over the characters below!

S.O.S.
Stuck in a tree house, like Jack was – and need to send a message to someone? Don't worry – this book can help!
STEP #1: Write your note on the back of the next page.
STEP #2: Carefully remove the page with a trusty pair of scissors.
STEP #3: Fold it into a paper airplane.
STEP #4: Launch that sucker!

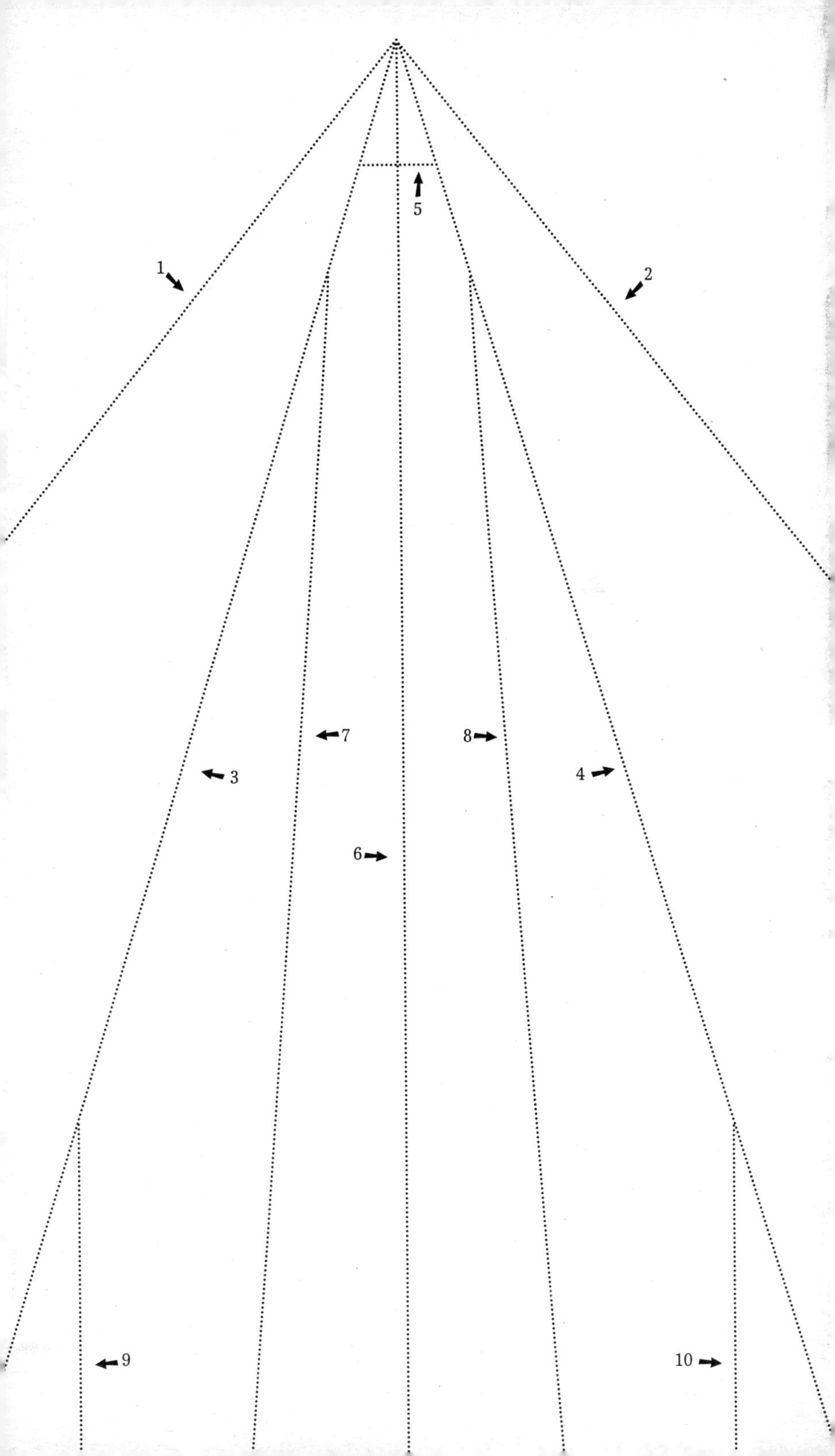

1
2
5
7
8
3
4
6
9
10

Help!

WRITE YOUR PAPER AEROPLANE NOTE HERE!

YOUR OWN PLAYLIST!

It's no secret that June loves music. What are your seven favourite jams? Bonus points for songs that you listen to while reading *The Last Kids on Earth*!

Today's Date: ______________________

1) ______________________

2) ______________________

3) ______________________

4) ______________________

5) ______________________

6) ______________________

7) ______________________

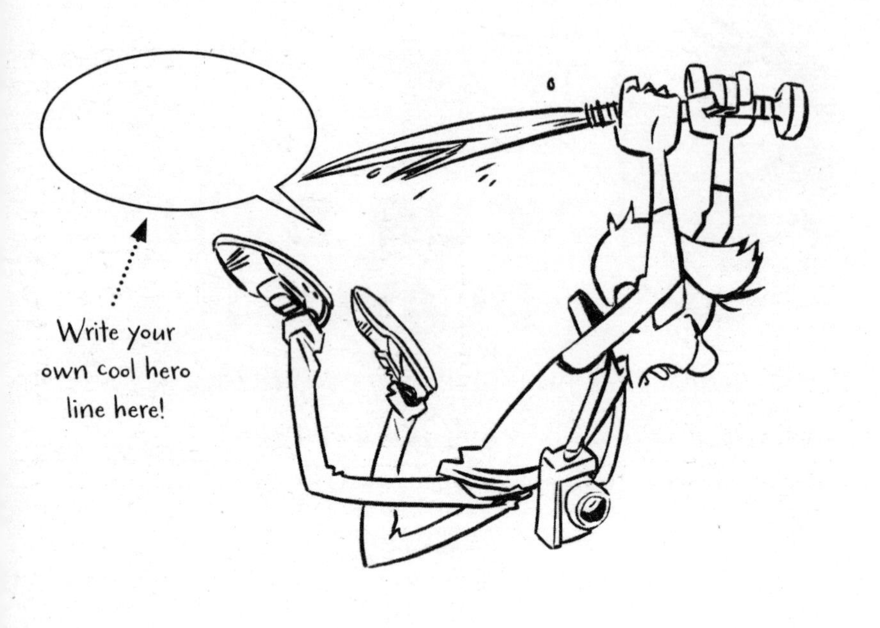
Write your own cool hero line here!

IT'S COLOURIN' TIME!

HEROIC ONE-LINERS!

Jack has said some pretty killer things to monsters. Write down some heroic stuff you would say if you were staring down a big beastie! Some of Jack's better lines . . .

"Hey! Monster face! Get a life!"
"Let's dance, monster pants!"
"No one messes with Earth on my watch!"

YOUR OWN COOL LINES!

Rover is inspired by Max Brallier's childhood dog, Champ.

QUINT'S GADGETS AND GIZMOS

Salutations, friends! It is I, Quint! I hope you are enjoying your time with this whimsical tome. Please peruse my collection of gadgets. They may someday prove useful!

Glue Thrower, Goo Slower

Tactical Belt

Little Hug Monster-Stopping Juice Grenades

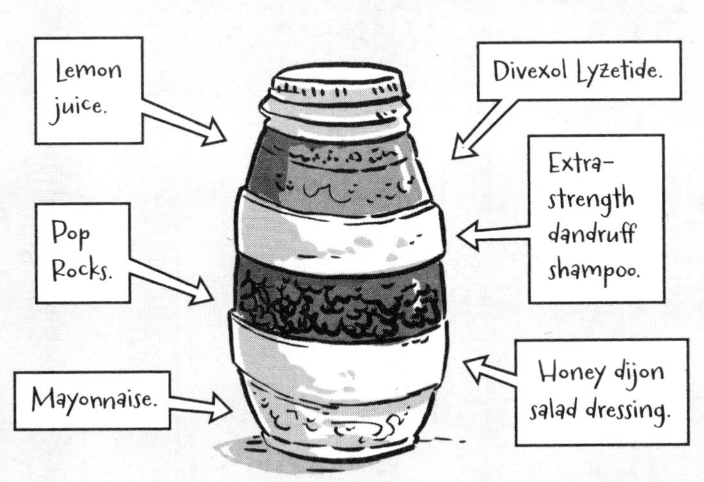

June Bait

The Scream Machine

The BOOMerang

(a weapon that goes boom)

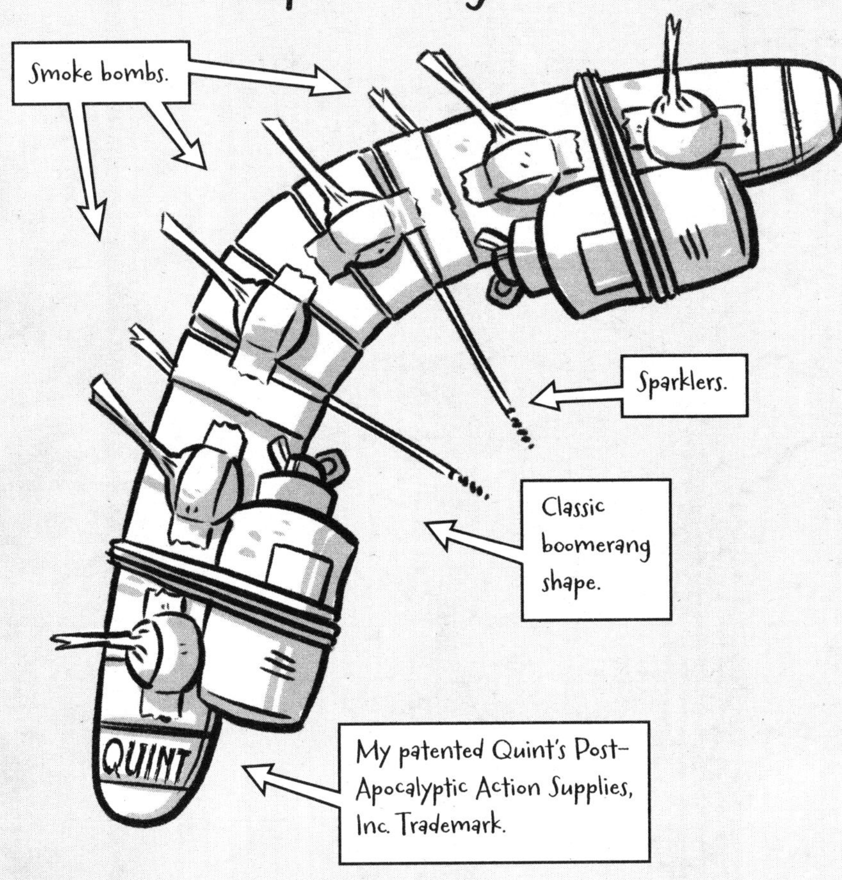

The first Last Kids on Earth book took Max Brallier nearly seven hundred days to write.

The following contraption is not for the faint of heart and should by no means be attempted at home, assuming your world has not yet been ravaged by zombie and/or monster hordes:

CREATE YOUR OWN QUINT GADGET!

Arrows and labels will prove useful.

QUINT'S WORKSHOP!
My workshop is now yours to command! Load it up with your own gadgets. Then label them – just like I do!

Meet Rover!

Fact Sheet!

- 3.5 metres high (6 when standing). 2.4 metres wide. 8.2 metre long, including tail. Quint estimates his weight at 2.5 tons.
- Two months after the Monster Apocalypse, Rover followed Jack home. He quickly became the pet 'dog' that Jack always wanted.
- Sometimes can almost sort of do tricks.
- Eats what he's supposed to fetch.
- Favourite snack is monster bones.

ARMOURED ROVER!
Reins, for steering.
Cute puppy-dog grin.
Teeth that could puncture Dozer skin.
Scars and battle wounds. Being Jack's mount can be a dangerous thing.

YOUR MONSTER PET

If you could have a pet monster like Rover, what sort of creature would you choose? Missile-breathing dragon? Zombified flamingo?

Design and draw it here!

What's your pet's awesome monster name?

What are your pet's cool abilities and powers?

What sort of tricks can your pet perform?

Dirk is inspired by both Wolverine and the Incredible Hulk – Max Brallier's favourite superheroes!

THE TREE HOUSE

The tree house is where Jack, June, Quint, Dirk, and Rover live! Quint and Dirk update its gadgets and defences, while Jack and June make sure it's a fun place to hang.

Catapult #1.

Zip line (great for last-minute escapes. Also for drying socks).

Cool guy.

Mountain Dew distillery (working on perfecting the formula – currently just hot dog water and green food colouring).

Toilet bucket.

TURN THE PAGE TO MAKE THE TREE HOUSE YOURS!

The tree house is yours – do what you want with it! Add hammocks, Velcro walls, a special zip line – *whatever you want!*

HOW TO DRAW ROVER

Get your doodle on!

1) Big oval for a big head! Place eyelines.

Don't forget to use a pencil, so you can erase mistakes!

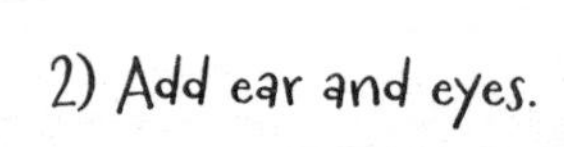

2) Add ear and eyes.

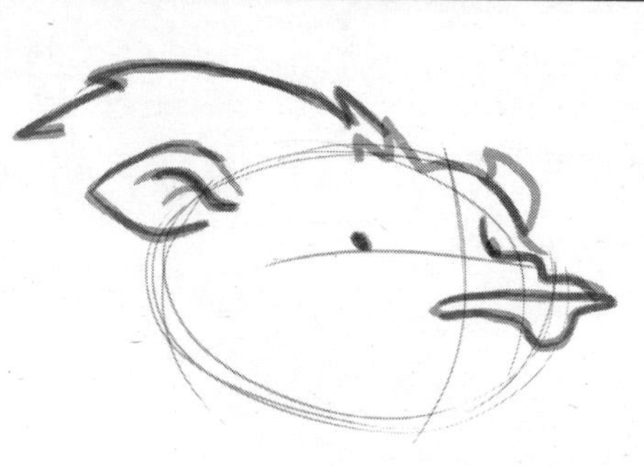

3) Add back of neck, other ear, snout and nose.

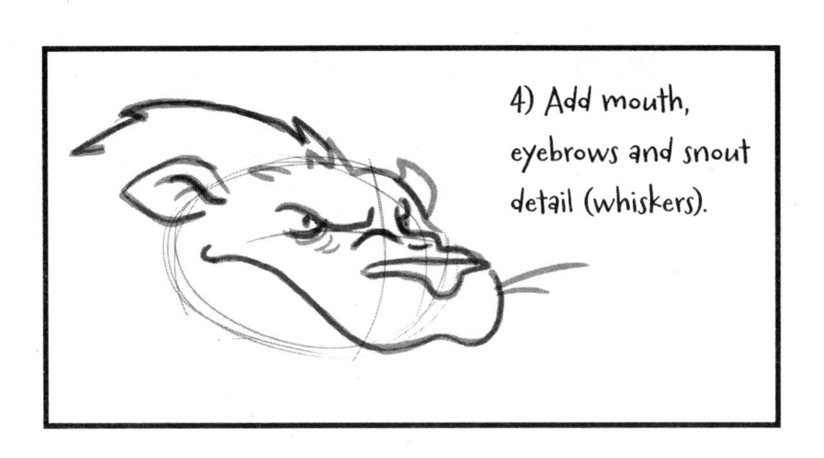
4) Add mouth,
eyebrows and snout
detail (whiskers).

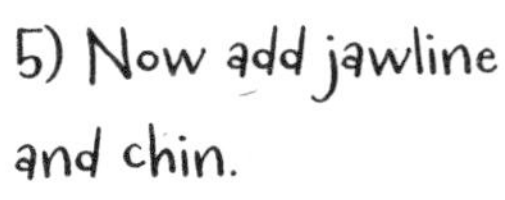
5) Now add jawline
and chin.

6) Teeth!
More fur!

TOOLS OF THE TRADE

Check out of some of our heroes' *most radical* tools. They take down big bad monsters and hold back zombie hordes.

THE GIFT THAT KEEPS ON BLASTING

JACK'S MOJO

Heavy-duty knuckles. You won't believe the stories they can tell!
PUNCH!
PUNCH!
PUNCH!
PUNCH!
PUNCH!
DIRK'S FISTS
POP
Boxing wraps, for optimal monster slugging.
Explosive Aero-Football.
TURBO CROSSBOW
Spare armaments container.
Bungee cord brace.

QUINT'S BRAIN

Cryptids.

Research!

Comic-Con.

Which came first: The chicken or the egg? The peanut butter or the jelly?

GIF or JIF?

Han shot first.

Legit Brain Stuff.

Egg salad.

Science!

Reese's.

FUN FACT:

Max Brallier's favourite movie of all time is *Star Wars*.

YOUR POST-APOCALYPTIC WEAPON

It's the end of the world, monsters and zombies are everywhere, and YOU need to survive!

Is your weapon big and intimidating? Or easily hidden in case of an action-hero surprise?

It's up to you! Go wild! Add arrows and labels to point out all the coolest parts!

Now tell us about this crazy thing!

And don't forget to give it a rad name!

IT'S COLOURIN Time!

Ultimate End-of-the-World Armour

Jack and his buddies have armoured up lots of times. Sometimes they grab stuff from around the house or school. Or sometimes it gets even more serious, like when Jack stepped inside the space marine armour from his favourite game:

TURN THE PAGE TO DESIGN YOUR ARMOUR!

Make up your own crazy armour!

Oh, hey!
That's pretty
neat armour!
Armour notes:

Punch-buggy, neon green!
TOUGH GUYS
Um, pretty sure that's just monster guts from last week's 'incident.'
Aw, man.
BIG MAMA
The Post-Apocalyptic Ride
Arrow turret.
Bottle-rocket launchers.
Fuzzy mice (for science).
Many, many, many boxes of Brown Sugar Cinnamon Pop-Tarts.
Storage for loot nabbed from Best Buy.
Reinforced windows keep zombies out.
Hitch for Rover's side car (side car still being built).
Tyre chains, for rolling over monsters.

TURN THE PAGE TO DESIGN YOUR VEHICLE!

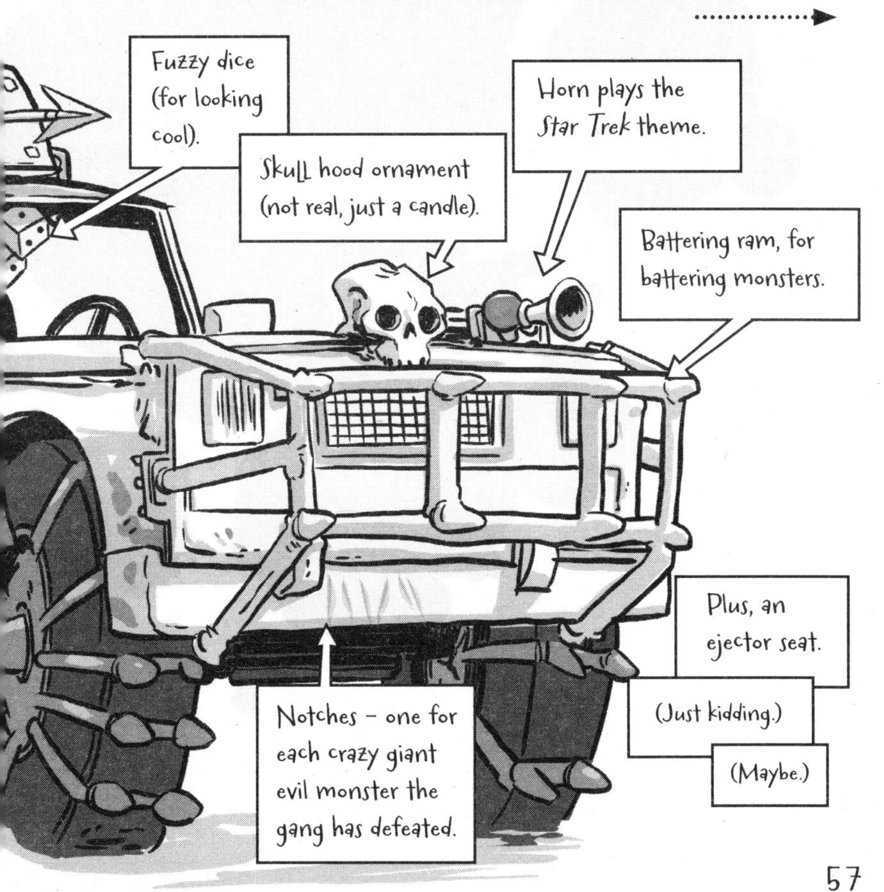

Design Your Own End-of-the-World Vehicle!

Big Mama is rad – but you can do better! It's time to create the coolest vehicle ever, period, no limits. GO!

BOOMKART BONANZA!

BoomKarts are souped-up bumper cars designed for vehicular combat coolness. Quint added paintball blasters, defensive marble spillers, spiked tyres, gas-powered slingshots and more!

NOW IT'S YOUR TURN!

Draw your own – with gadgets, weapons, armour, and defences. Is it built for speed or built for battling monsters? You decide!

Design your own BoomKart track!

Imagine your neighbourhood or your school – then turn it into a racetrack! Add twists, turns, drops, dead ends, drawbridges, tunnels, zombies, monsters – anything goes!

HOW TO DRAW JACK

1) Draw an oval and eyelines.

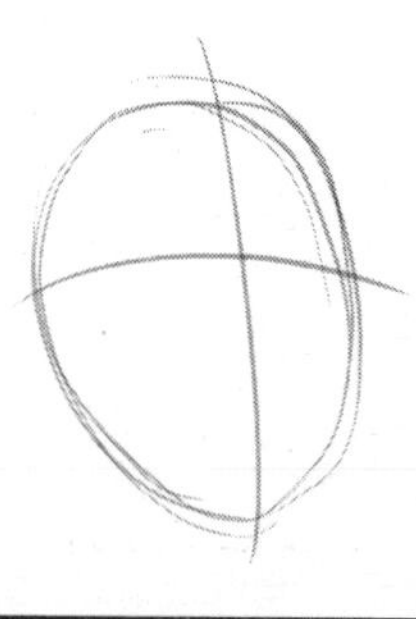

2) Add eyes and ears.

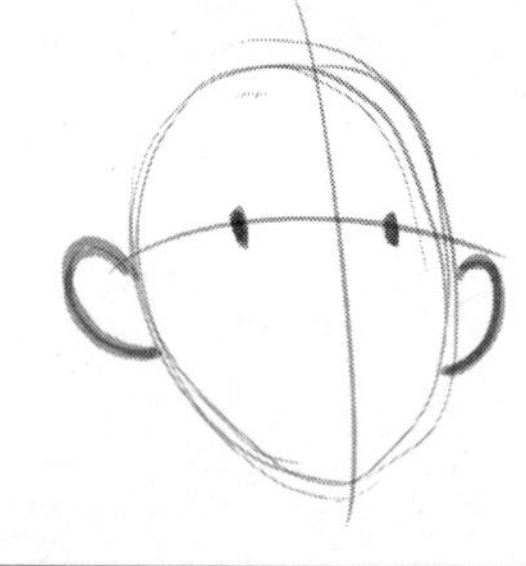

3) Lots of curly lines: add nose, eyebrows, and ear detail.

4) Add Sydney Opera House sails for hair!*

5) Define chin and add grin!

*EDITOR'S NOTE: Douglas Holgate is from Australia, and the Sydney Opera House is a cool reference.

Your Own Last Kids on Earth Book!

You get to be the author! What are the biggest parts of your original Last Kids adventure? Be sure to add gadgets and danger!

Who's the bad guy? ______________________

____

____

What's the scariest thing that happens? ______________________

____

____

____

What's the funniest thing that happens? ______________________

____

____

____

____

____

Draw some Douglas Holgate-style cover art!

MEET THE MONSTERS!

EVIL BEASTS, FRIENDLY DUDES, AND IN-BETWEEN ONES!

THE MONSTERS OF JOE'S PIZZA

Good-guy monsters took up residence here in Wakefield Town Square – and things haven't been the same since! They're buddies with Jack and friends, and they've battled alongside them.

Bardle is wizened, wizardly, and wise. He's an advisor to Jack and the human heroes – passing on knowledge about monsters, the ultimate evil bad dude, Ŗeżżőcħ, and life in the monster dimension. . . .

Skaelka was a vicious warrior in the monster dimension. She is scary savage and fiercely ferocious. In fact, she's kind of obsessed with chopping off bad guy heads – although Jack always seems to stop her at the last moment.

-Biggun-

Check this out: one time, Dirk and Jack turned this huge monster into a rideable beast by strapping shopping carts to his back. He became 'The Biggun Mobile'.

ŖEŻŻŐCH: THE BIG BAD

Ŗeżżőch the Ancient, Destructor of Worlds is the ultimate ultra-villain! He comes from the time before time, when great battles were fought in the monster dimension. . .

We have not yet seen Ŗeżżőcħ here on Earth. Draw what YOU think this otherworldly evil might look like.

Warg isn't like the other monsters. All Jack and his pals know is that she's got a weird eyeball body and she's full of secrets. . . .

EYEBALL POWERS!

What if you controlled an army of eyeballs like Warg? List some people you would spy on! Teachers? Siblings? Weirdo neighbours? Parents? Other random old people? List ten things you would do!

1) ______________________________

2) ______________________________

3) ______________________________

4) ______________________________

5) ______________________________

6) ______________________________

7) ______________________________

8) ______________________________

9) ______________________________

10) ______________________________

SPOT THE DIFFERENCE!

Check out the two pictures of Jack taking an apocalyptic morning stroll below. There are ten differences between the two – can you find all of them?

JOE'S PIZZA'S NEWEST MONSTER!

Draw and design a new good-guy monster who can hang out at Joe's Pizza!

MONSTER'S NAME: ____________________

Weapon: ____________________

Monster's special power: ____________________

Ten fun facts about your monster:

1) ____________________

2) ____________________

3) ____________________

4) ____________________

5) ____________________

6) ____________________

7) ____________________

8) ____________________

9) ____________________

10) ____________________

Make Your Own Joe's Pizza Menu!

Your customers are monsters! Don't forget, monsters eat weird stuff like tongues, spiders (dead and alive), eyeballs and creepy-crawly critters!

PIZZA TOPPINGS:

STARTERS:

DRINKS & LIQUIDS:

DESSERT & GELATO:

UNDER NEW MANAGEMENT

Cooking with Bardle

FIND OUT THIS AND MORE WHEN YOU SUBSCRIBE TO MY YOUTUBE CHANNEL AND PODCAST * – MONSTER MEAL PREPARATION ON AN INTESTINE-STRING BUDGET.

*Internet no longer exists, thanks to Monster-Zombie Apocalypse.

Recipe:
BUGS ON A LOG

1) SPREAD SOME PEANUT BUTTER ON CELERY THAT YOUR PARENTS HAVE CUT FOR YOU OR THAT CAME ALREADY CUT FROM THE GROCERY STORE.

2) PLACE RAISINS ON TOP TO TASTE. LIVE BUGS ARE ALSO ACCEPTABLE, BUT THEY MAY CRAWL AWAY IF THEY DON'T STICK TO THE PEANUT BUTTER.

3) IF USING RAISINS, DO NOT SERVE TO BIGGUN, AS HE IS HIGHLY ALLERGIC. MONSTER SKIN ALLERGIES ARE FRIGHTENING TO BEHOLD, EVEN TO THOSE WITH THE STEELIEST CONSTITUTIONS.

Max Brallier's second favourite movie is *Indiana Jones and the Temple of Doom*.

OTHER MONSTERS!

There are monsters in Wakefield that Jack and his buddies don't even know! Name 'em! Write about 'em! Add fun facts!

NAME: ______________________________

FUN FACTS:

____

____

____

____

____

____

____

____

____

NAME: ______________________________

FUN FACTS:

____

____

____

____

____

NAME: ____________________

FUN FACTS:

____

____

FUN FACTS:

FUN FACT:

When he was a kid, Max had a tree house in his backyard. It wasn't fancy, but it did have a zip line!

HOW TO DRAW BARDLE

1) Draw circle for top of the head, place eyeline and nose guides.

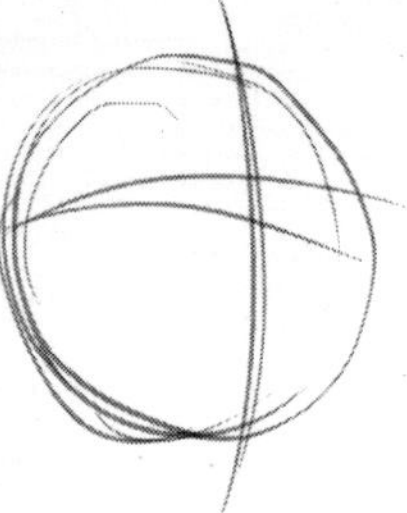

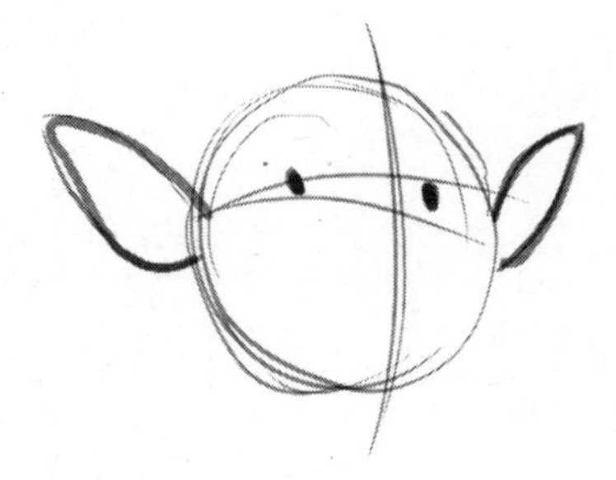

2) Add ears and eyes. Be sure to leave plenty of room for his mouth and beard!

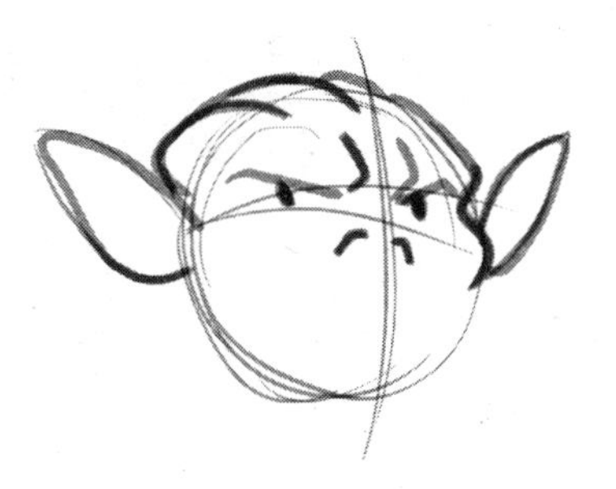

3) Add stern eyebrows, nostrils and bumpy scalp!

4) Add earrings, cheekbones and the start of the moustache.

5) Finish beard, add shoulders and mighty sword hilt!

ZOMBIFY THE HEROES!

It's time for Jack, June, Dirk and Quint to get ZOMBIFIED! Trace over the lines and give them lots of ghoulish features – the grosser, the better!

Creepy zombie-dudes in case you need inspiration!

IT'S COLOURIN' TIME!

Thrull Interrogates Author Max Brallier!

Thrull first appeared as a tough warrior and monster hunter. But in fact, he was secretly working as a servant of Ŗeżżőcħ, manipulating Jack in order to bring Ŗeżżőcħ to this world. Now he's back, and he's got some questions.

Thrull: First, why the name Thrull?

Max: I wanted to do Krull, but then I realised *I* didn't invent that name – it's from the movie *Krull*. So I made up a new name that sounded like it: THRULL!

Thrull: Second, why the name Max?

Max: Ask my parents! All I know is, when I was a kid, I never met anyone else named Max. The only Maxs were dogs. Everyone was like, 'Oh, I have a dog named Max, it's a great name for a dog, yadda yadda yadda.' I was like, yeah, cool, whatever, but I'm a human, and I think it's a fine name for a human.

Thrull: Are you Jack?

Max: No, I'm Max. But am I like Jack? Sorta. . . Jack's like the cool, brave, funny version of me. I'm like the dorky, geeky version of Jack – which is saying a lot, because Jack is already super dorky and super geeky.

Thrull: Why did you make me so monstrous and evil? Not sure how I feel about that.

Max: Someone's gotta be the bad dude. Just happens that I made that someone you.

Thrull: Why couldn't you make me clever, like Quint?

Max: You *are* clever! You had that whole clever plan with the bestiary! I mean, I think and hope it was clever – I wrote it, and it seemed like a clever bad-guy plan to me!

Thrull: What scares you?

Max: Lots of stuff. Rats, mice, snakes, heights, the deep deep ocean, deep deep space – also missing deadlines and bad reviews of my books.

Thrull: How come I can never put Jack in his place like June does?

Max: June's tougher and cooler than you. Sorry – it's just a fact, dude.

Thrull: Where do you write my tales of adventure? Office, poolside, cabin, tree house?

Max: First of all, they aren't *your* tales of adventure –

you're the bad guy! But to answer the actual question, I do most of my writing in coffee shops in New York City and in restaurants on the road.

Thrull: How do you write? Pen, typewriter, computer?

Max: I use a blue pen and a notebook to jot down ideas, because I get ideas everywhere. I even had the idea for you in the shower – true story! When it's time to write the real book, I use a computer.

Thrull: Do you describe the characters to Douglas Holgate? Tell him what they look like? Or does he read the book and then come up with how they look? What did you tell him about me? I'm really better looking than this, you know.

Max: A bit of both. Basically, I write a few dinky words, then Doug takes those few dinky words and turns them into something pure awesome. And you he made pure evil.

Thrull: Do you know right now what's going to happen in, like, books six, seven, twenty?

Max: Yes and no. I've got a plan for the grand finale, and I've got a few ideas for what happens along the way. Each book will continue to feel bigger and more epic. And I want to see the heroes fail a bunch of times – I don't want them to just win, win, win.

Thrull: What's it like to be a human? If living isn't all about destroying Earth, what do you do all day? I don't get that.

Max: I play ping-pong, ride my bike, play video games, read books, sit on my butt, take photos, daydream and hang with my family.

Thrull: How do the books end? Do the heroes survive? Find happiness? Do I?

Max: You'll have to wait and see! I'll tell you this much, though: I hate when endings are totally perfect and happy. I like a little bit of sadness and loss – even in a happy ending.

Thrull: Why did you make my personality so, well, wooden? And don't cop out and blame it on your editor.

Max: Oh, I get it – it's a joke, because of the tree thing*? Ha. Ha. Very funny.

Thrull: Why did you ever think loud music would distract me from my evil plot? What is wrong with you?

Max: It worked, didn't it?

Thrull: Will Jack and June ever kiss?

Max: Dude! None of your business! I'm out – this interview is *over*!

*

A VILLAINOUS NEW SPECIES!

Dozers, Vine-Thingies and Winged Wretches are, like, their own categories of monster. Create your own species!

SPECIES NAME: ______________________________

MAIN ATTACK: ______________________________

____

BIGGEST WEAKNESS: ______________________________

____

____

WEIRD FACTS: ______________________________

____

____

____

____

____

____

YOUR VERY OWN COSMIC SERVANT

Ŗeżżőcħ's Cosmic Servants are the BIGGEST and BADDEST monsters – like Blarg, Thrull and the King Wretch. Design your own here!

What is the Cosmic Servant's name? ____________________

____

What are its evil powers? ____________________

____

What is the scariest thing about this monster? ____________

____

____

What is the grossest thing about this monster? ____________

____

____

____

What would you do if YOU encountered this creature?

____

____

____

____

Zombify a Buddy!

Draw friends or family members or even pets – but zombify them! To get extra weird, tape a photo of them here and draw all over them!

MONSTER LANGUAGE DECODED!

Quint got his hands on Bardle's private notebook, and it turns out he writes in a completely different monster language!

Use the code below to write secret messages to your buddies in Bardle speak! Make photocopies of the code for your friends so you can trade messages.

HOW TO DRAW EVIE

She's a fiend! Let's learn how to draw her anyway!

1) Draw oval and eyelines.

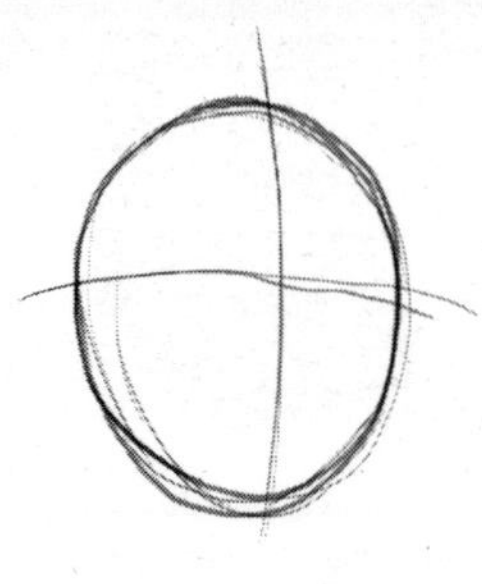

Be sure to leave room for her hair – it's pretty big!

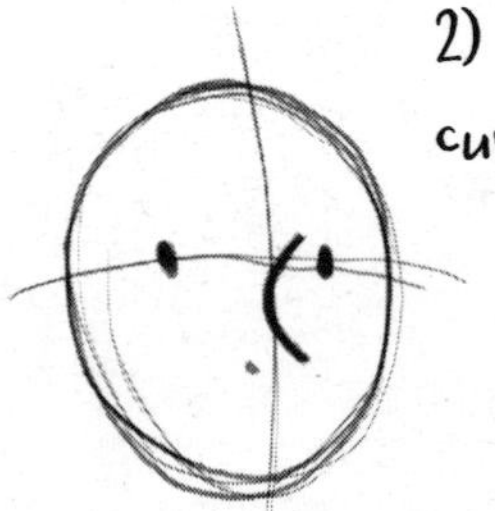

2) Add eyes and curved nose.

3) Add eyebrows and ears.

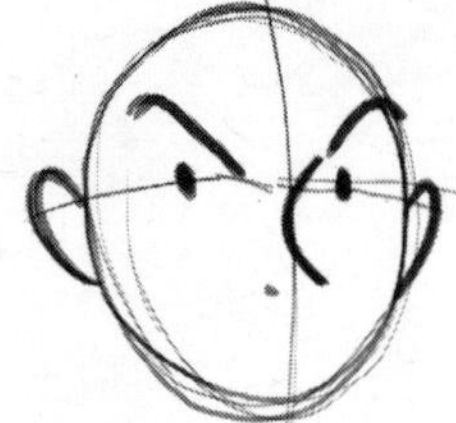

4) Define chin.
Add evil grin and
ear detail.

5) Add wild hair!
Make sure you
add extra curls!

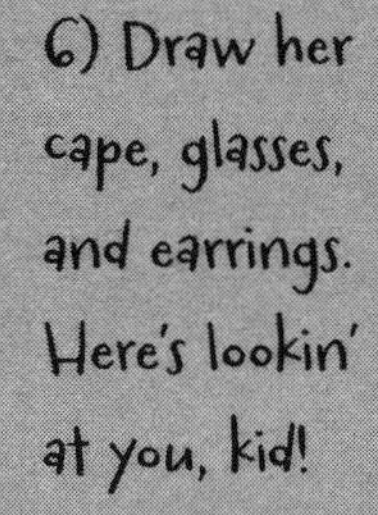

6) Draw her
cape, glasses,
and earrings.
Here's lookin'
at you, kid!

Max Brallier sometimes writes under a different name: Jack Chabert.

HAVING FUN DURING THE MONSTER-ZOMBIE APOCALYPSE

(I MEAN, IT'S NOT LIKE THE
WORLD IS ENDING, RIGHT?)

. . . THE GAME!

Jack and Quint love video games. Their favourite is the space marine shooter *Nimbus: Call to Action*.

Imagine you could create your own video game about the Last Kids on Earth!

What's the title? ____________________

____

What type of game is it? ____________________

____

____

Who's the big final boss at the end of the game? ________

____

____

What vehicles do the characters use? ______________________

____

What's the best part of the game? ______________________

____

____

____

____

____

____

TURN THE PAGE TO DESIGN
YOUR GAME'S COVER! ···············►

A good video game needs a good cover. Draw some awesome art for your Last Kids on Earth game!

Jack made his very own Licence to Kill Monsters card – and it was kind of lame.

But here is an actually awesome licence that you can cut out and carry with you!

cut here!

Don't leave home without it!
OFFICIAL MEMBERSHIP CARD
THIS WILL CERTIFY THAT THE BEARER OF THIS CARD IS AUTHORISED TO DESTROY MONSTERS & ZOMBIES WITH IMPUNITY
(Sign here to be an official member of the LAST KIDS fan club)
THE LAST KIDS ON EARTH

The Last Kids on Earth theme song!

Our heroes have a rad tree house, a mighty pet, and a crazy vehicle. But they don't have a theme song . . . yet.

Write some killer lyrics and give the gang the awesome theme song they deserve.

ICEE
Three MINUTES to GO!
The monster-zombie apocalypse has just begun!
You have only THREE MINUTES at your house.
What are you going to grab? Go!
And what about school? What will you take?
Heads up, guys! Be prepared.
Food, weapons, stuff to communicate with. And maybe a change of underwear!

To make it extra hard, try grabbing only things you can see from where you're sitting.

Things to grab from home: ______________________

____

____

____

____

____

Things to grab from school: ______________________

____

____

____

____

Peace out, y'all!

Your Monster-Zombie Apocalypse Plan!

If monsters and zombies come – what's your plan? Will you retreat to a hangout like Jack in the tree house? Or will you hop into a vehicle like Big Mama and get out of town? Write down your plans!

A Last Kids on Earth comic?
THAT'S WHAT'S UP!

Write and draw your own comic starring Jack, June, Quint, Dirk and Rover!

But meanwhile . . .

Soon . . .

Suddenly . . .

And then:

Uh-oh.

And that's
THE END
of that!

Jack looks at life like a video game — and video games have challenges you complete to earn trophies and achievements. Jack created his own. They are . . .

Feats of Apocalyptic Success!

FEAT: Mad Hatter!

Steal the hats off five zombies.

FEAT: Outrun!

Beat a zombie in a footrace.

FEAT: Say Cheese!

Take a photo with someone you knew before they got zombified.

FEAT: House Hunter

Explore 50 different abandoned houses.

FEAT: Get an Awesome Pet

Rover. 'Nuff said!

Your OWN Feats of Apocalyptic Success!

What if you were alone in a world of zombies, monsters, and buddies? What Feats of Apocalyptic Success would you create? Title them, describe them and draw some worthy badges!

FEAT: ______________________

____

FEAT: ______________________

____

FEAT: ______________________

____

FEAT:
FEAT:
FEAT:
It's cool, I get it – I'm an inspiration. But you gotta come up with your own!

Feats of Everyday Success!

Your real life may not be as action-packed as Jack's – but you can still create rad feats! Create everyday life challenges that you're going to complete!

FEAT: ______________________

____

FEAT: ______________________

____

FEAT: ______________________

____

FEAT: ______________________

____

FEAT: ______________________

____

FEAT: ______________________

____

Closet organising: Status – COMPLETE!

List-A-Rama!

Jack tries to help the monsters understand Earth. It's time to list the things that YOU would recommend to someone new to this dimension.

List 10 movies a new friend must watch:

1) ______________________________

2) ______________________________

3) ______________________________

4) ______________________________

5) ______________________________

6) ______________________________

7) ______________________________

8) ______________________________

9) ______________________________

10) ______________________________

Just like our heroes, Max went to Parker Middle School. But there were no zombies.

10 books a new friend must read:

1) ______

2) ______

3) ______

4) ______

5) ______

6) ______

7) ______

8) ______

9) ______

10) ______

10 games or activities a new friend must try:

1) ______________________________

2) ______________________________

3) ______________________________

4) ______________________________

5) ______________________________

6) ______________________________

7) ______________________________

8) ______________________________

9) ______________________________

10) ______________________________

MONSTER-ZOMBIE PICNIC!

When the gang had a picnic to scope out monster territory, they brought Quint's vintage lunch box, loaded with Reese's Pieces.

What would YOU pack for the perfect post-apocalyptic picnic hangout with your buddies?

LIST OR DRAW YOUR MONSTER-ZOMBIE PICNIC SNACKS!

Max owns more than one hundred vintage Star Wars toys and action figures. Yep, he's *super* cool.

WHAT'S YOUR POST-APOCALYPTIC MONSTER NAME?

First letter of your FIRST NAME

A – grub
B – beetle
C – terrible
D – bunion
E – stale
F – whiskery
G – stingy
H – X-ray
I – bitter
J – spotted
K – knuckle
L – sour
M –claw
N – gooey
O – voracious
P – repugnant
Q – toenail
R – elbow
S – tentacle
T – captain
U – hairy
V – stormy
W – crusty
X – wicked
Y – wartomous
Z – onion

First letter of your LAST NAME

A – menace
B – slime
C – boil
D – grimace
E – puke bug
F – snail
G – vomit
H – brains
I – breath
J – crusher
K – mud
L – roach
M – eggs
N – quicksand
O – demon
P – earwax
Q – vine
R – wormongulous
S – sludge
T – poison
U – eyeball
V – king
W – savage
X – sawtooth
Y – explosion
Z – sparkle

HELLO
my monster name is

CREATE YOUR OWN HOLIDAY!

Jack and his pals created their very own post-apocalyptic Christmas. They started new traditions, like a dance showdown, a wrapping paper sword duel and a king of the hill battle. Now it's your turn to create your own holiday!

What's it called? ____________________

What's being celebrated? ____________________

____

How often do you celebrate? ____________________

____

____

What's the BEST part of your holiday?

____

____

Are there awesome parts of other holidays that you'll throw into your totally original holiday?

Are there gifts? Or fireworks? OR BOTH?!

What are the traditions?

THE BESTIARY

Jack and his buddies catalogue and research the many monsters that have taken up residence in Wakefield. Turn the page to see what they've learned. . . .

CLASSIC ZOMBIE
(Undeadius Reanimatedus)

ZOMBIE BALL
(Undeadius Rollaroundus)

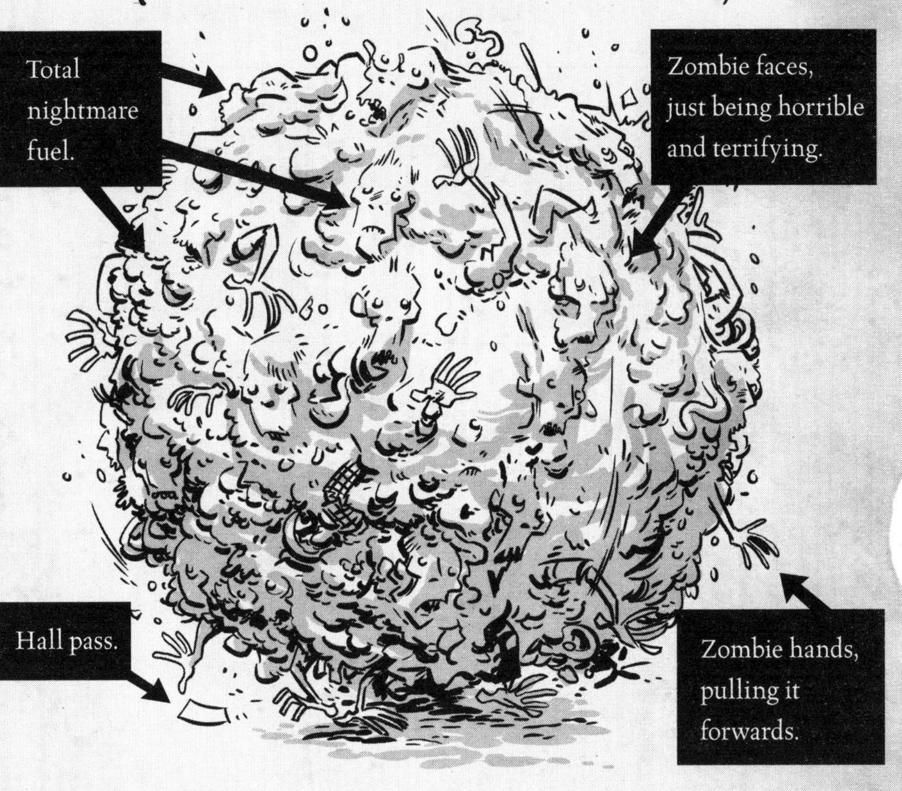

Quint Notes: A lurching mass of the undead; possibly created by one zombie tripping down the stairs and taking every zombie with him, snowball style.

Known Habitats: School, near the teacher's lounge.

Principal Attack: Rolling aimlessly, like a bitey tumbleweed.

Strengths: Flattening momentum.

Weaknesses: Doors, small hallways, turnstiles.

Hairy Eyeball Monster

(*Pilosus Acutus Oculus*)

Pupil opens to allow monster verbal communication (roars, shrieks, howls).

Iris colour changes depending on mood, weather.

One single, massive eyeball.

When angered, hair stands on end, forming razor-sharp quills.

Quint Notes: Ability to launch its quills at an enemy with crossbow force, distance and accuracy.

Known Habitats: Old South Graveyard.

Principal Attack: Needle onslaught.

Strengths: Rolling ability makes for easy, unobstructed travel and pursuit. Undefeated at staring contests.

Weaknesses: Bright flashes, moderate ragweed allergy, contact lenses.

LITTLE GUYS
(*Tinius Furrius*)

PUKE BUG KING

(Rex Putidus Insectus)

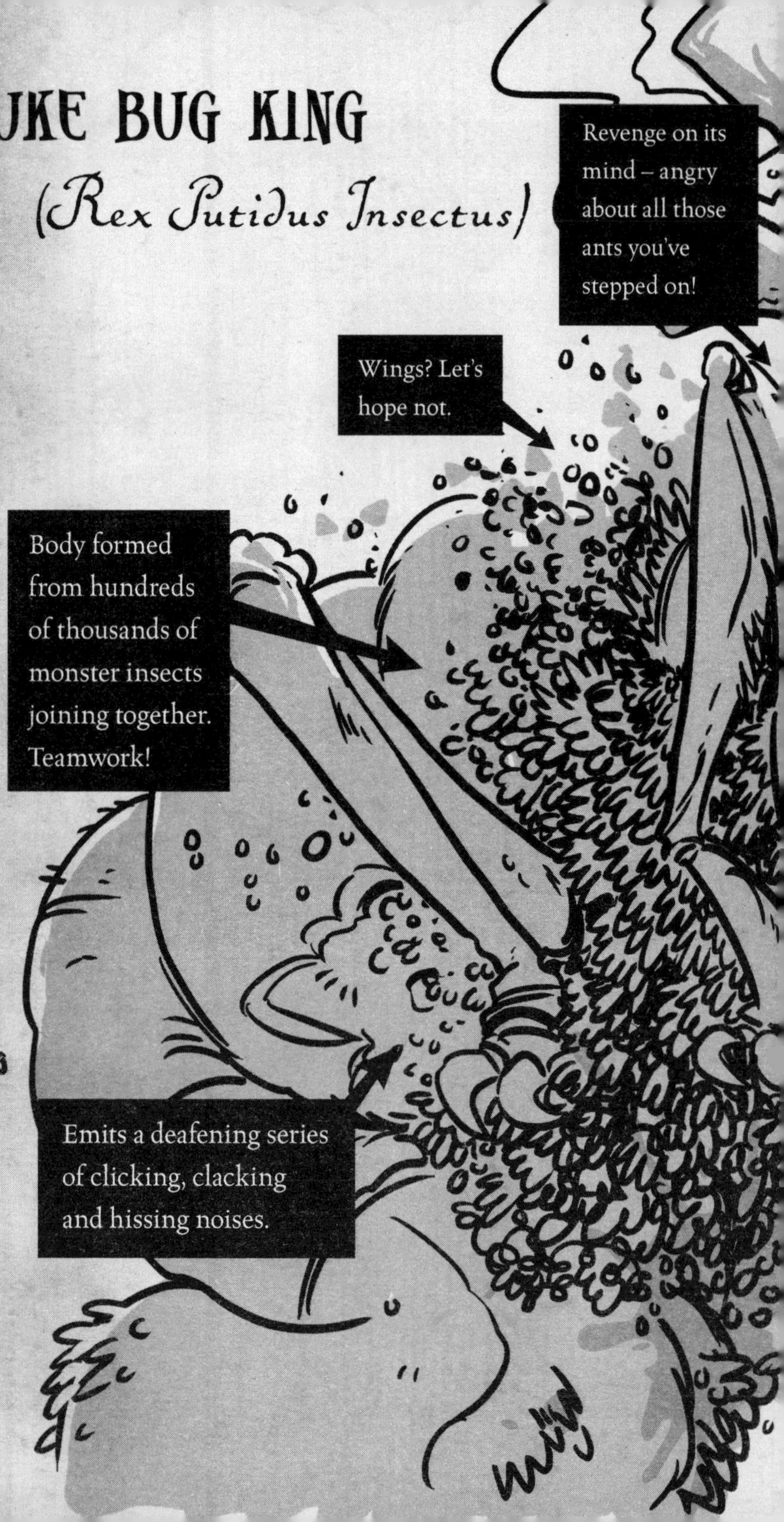

Revenge on its mind – angry about all those ants you've stepped on!

Wings? Let's hope not.

Body formed from hundreds of thousands of monster insects joining together. Teamwork!

Emits a deafening series of clicking, clacking and hissing noises.

Releases a sweet, overpowering stench.

Facial features evident.

Quint Notes: A slew of tiny, monstrous insects, formed together to create a 'King Bug'. P.B.K.'s brain is as yet unknown.

Known Habitats: June's neighbours' house (the Gradwohls).

Principal Attack: Crushing YOU like a bug, for once.

Strengths: Unbreakable shell – is anything stronger than a gulbillion exoskeletons acting as one?!

Weaknesses: Citronella-and-bug-spray flamethrower.

BLARG
(*Blargus*)

40 feet tall.

Armoured skin.

Teeth on teeth on teeth on TEETH.

Smells like 3-day-old barf.

Clawed hands – y'know, for clawing stuff.

Disgusting tentacles.

Action hero
leap pose!
Don't try at
home.
Acid bubbling on
forehead wound.
See?! Toldya
about the teeth.
ACID BLARG
(Blargus Acetous)
Look on his face
like, 'THIS TIME
IT'S PERSONAL!'

DOZER *(Bula Ploeg)*

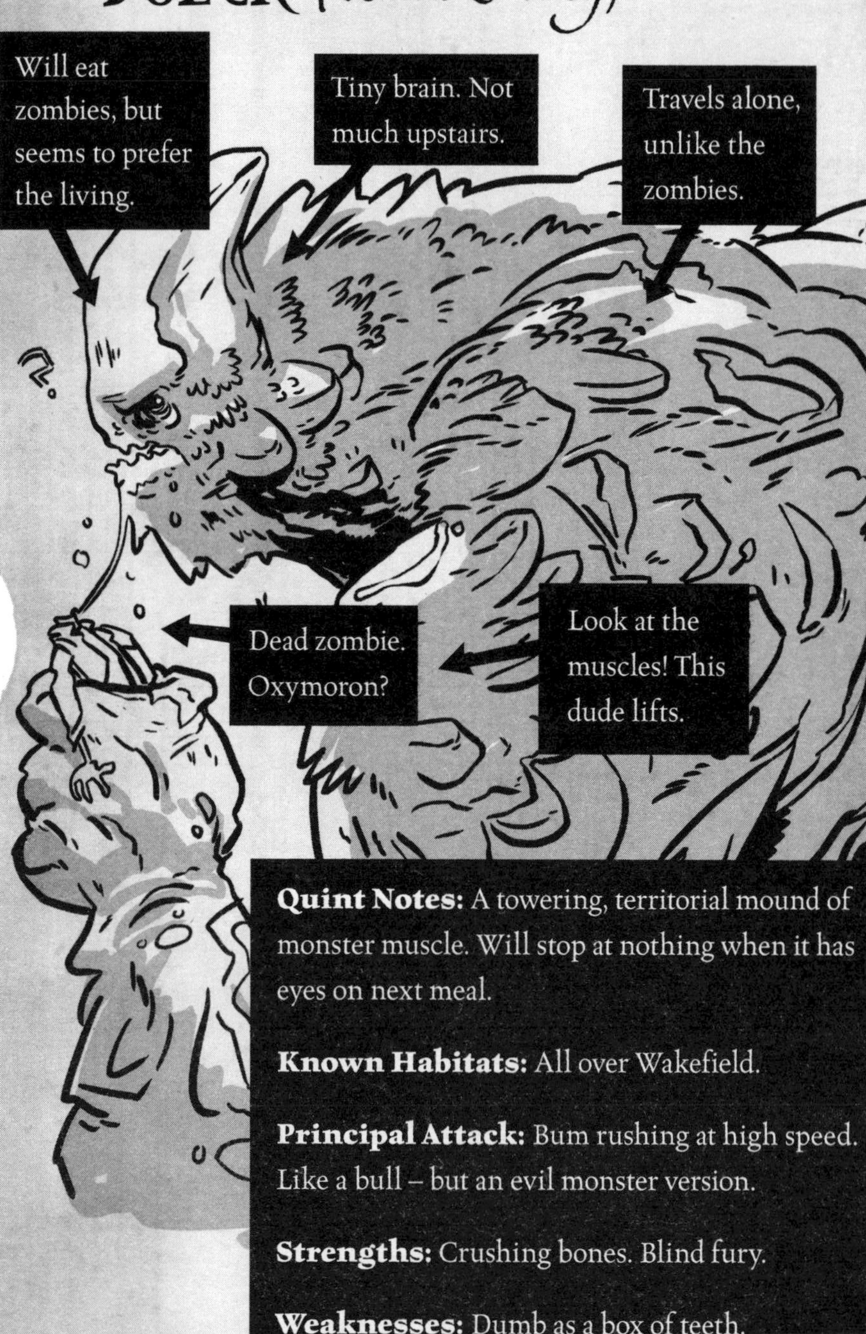

Quint Notes: A towering, territorial mound of monster muscle. Will stop at nothing when it has eyes on next meal.

Known Habitats: All over Wakefield.

Principal Attack: Bum rushing at high speed. Like a bull – but an evil monster version.

Strengths: Crushing bones. Blind fury.

Weaknesses: Dumb as a box of teeth.

Aerodynamic wings for diving on prey crazy fast.
Super long swivel neck for 360 degree hunting.
WINGED WRETCH
(Wretchedus Wingdum)
Fun to trim!
VINE-THINGIES
(Vinus Thingamabobus)
Grow everywhere! What do they want?!

THRULL
(Tradere Vilis)

Radical hammer-club-mallet dealie.

Generally humanoid face.

Cologne stench.

Absolutely CRUSHING No-Shave November.

Compasses, gizmos and beastly thingamabobs.

Fang necklace. So you know he's mean.

Opposable thumbs.

Bone and skull jewellery (probably not a good sign).

Horrific eyeholes clawed from bark.

Evil stench emanating!

Still rocking the radical beard!

Vine-Thingies covering his body .

Woody tree-trunk legs.

THRULL THE TREE BEAST

(Vilis Deku Woodenus)

THE KING WRETCH

(Wretchedus Rex)

Quint Notes: The alpha Wretch; much bigger than an average Wretch and much stronger. Best described as 'nightmare fuel'.

Known Habitats: High above Wakefield; Comically Speaking.

Principal Attack: Hypnosis, followed by talon-grab 'n' smash.

Strengths: Telepathy, flight, breakneck speed, general terror-inducing.

Weaknesses: The Scrapken.

Battle scars.

Bone wings.

Ginormous jaws.
Freaky-deaky swirly eyeballs.
Bloodcurdling action pose.
Razor-sharp talons.

WORMUNGULOUS
(Graboidous)

Quint Notes: Part millipede, part centipede, part earthworm, part freight train.
Known Habitats: The Circle One Mall
Principal Attack: Bursting out of the ground, jaws-first; earthquake flop.
Strengths: Stealth mode, skin like a tank.
Weaknesses: Poor eyesight. Bad at hiding.
Jaws like a rusty lawnmower.
Kinda squishy here! Might want tickles?

Cosmically bad intentions!

Strange, snapping, twitching tail.

GHAZT (Mighty Gnawus)

Action figure bits.

Face is part rat and part melted plastic – it's barforama gnarly!
Giant action-figure limbs!
More action figure bits.

THE SCRAPKEN
(Junkcelcior Maximus)
'Just woke up' face.
One eye – which is one too many.
Quint Notes: Possesses many qualities of a kraken, but instead of water, it lives in trash.
Known Habitats: Big Al's Junkyard; perhaps elsewhere?
Principal Attack: Ripping enemies limb from limb.
Strengths: Multiple, tentacled limbs, the size of a city bus.
Weaknesses: He's a trash guy.

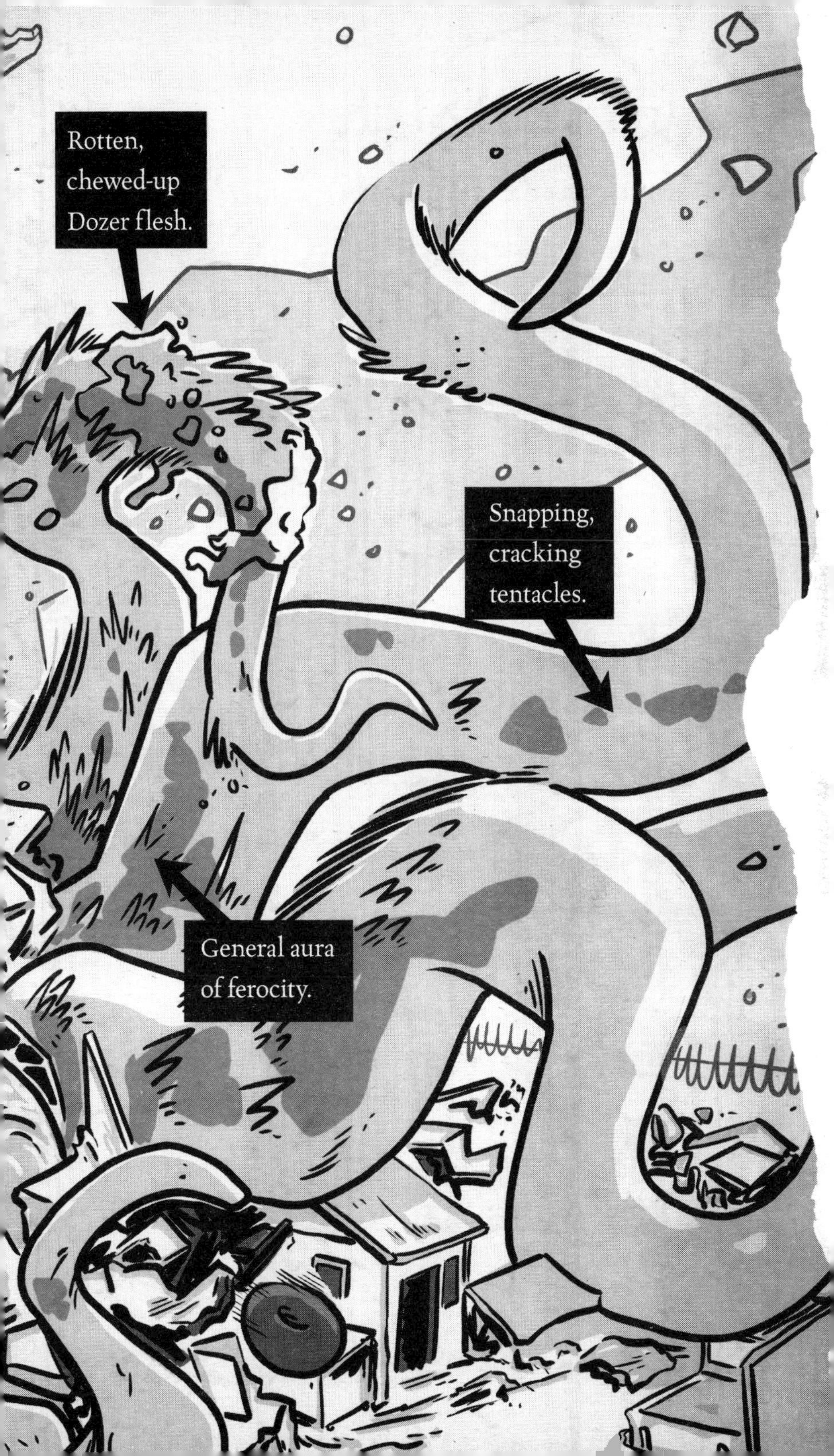
Rotten, chewed-up Dozer flesh.
Snapping, cracking tentacles.
General aura of ferocity.

UGLY MONSTER

(Only a Facex a Mother Could Lovus)

No eyes. Which just makes it freakier. . .

Gills for breathing, hearing and sensing.

Mouth cannot close – constantly drooling.

EWW, NAKED MONSTER!

Elbow blades.

Arm? Foot? Both?

SLUDGE SAVAGE
(Gelatinous Ferocious)

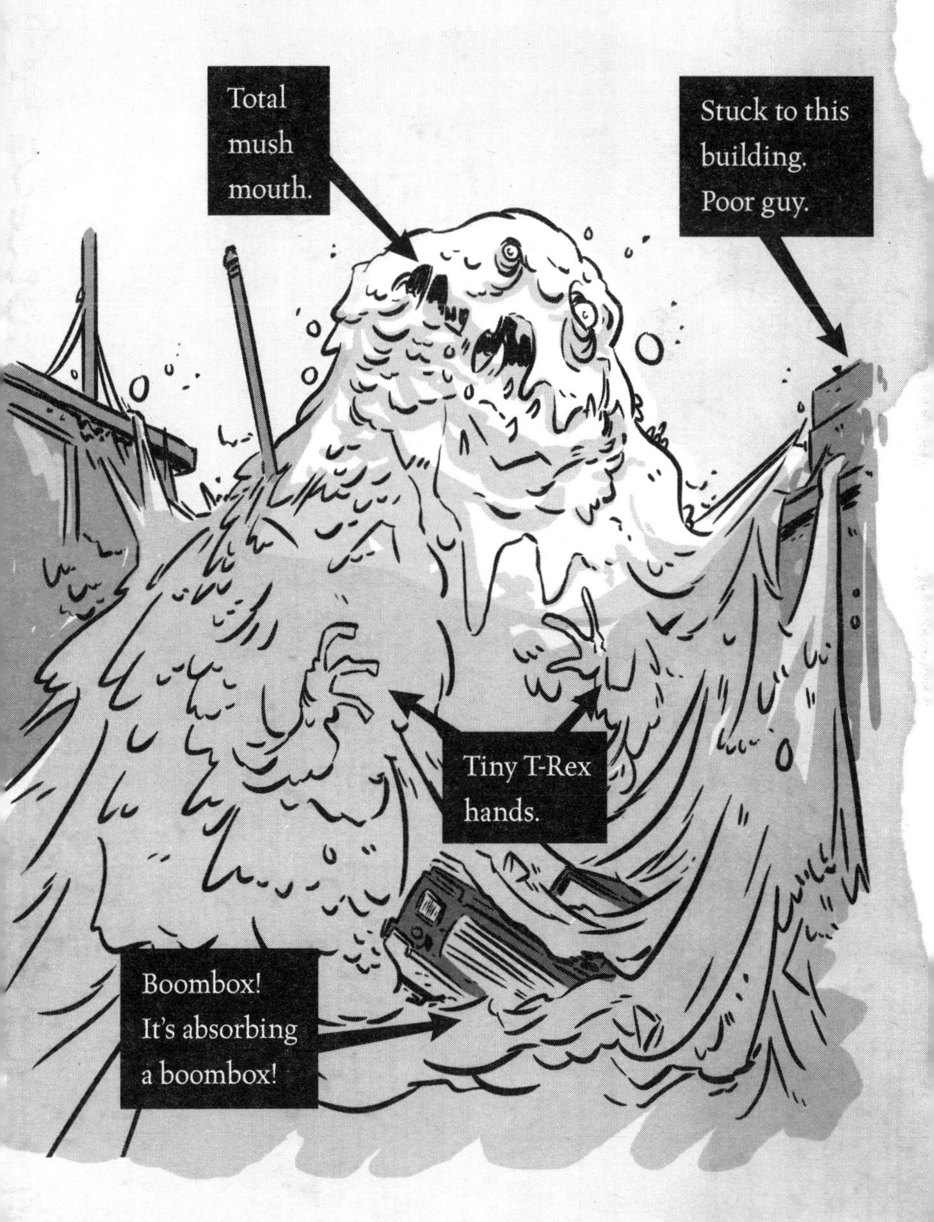

OIL MONSTER

(Fossilfuelus Prodigium)

MEATHOOK (*Hamburgo Cibum*)

BIG FIST! POWERFUL PAW! ACTION ARM!

Broken chains! Escaped beast?!

Mean, mean underbite.

Sliced-off arm – what battles has this dude been in?!

Uh-oh – looks like Jack and his friends skipped a few pages! It's up to *you* to complete the bestiary. Design three new monsters!

NAME:

Notes:

____

____

____

Known Habitats:

____

Principal Attack:

____

Strengths:

____

Weaknesses:

____

NAME:

Notes:

____

____

____

Known Habitats:

____

Principal Attack:

____

Strengths:

____

Weaknesses:

____

NAME:

Notes:

Known Habitats:

Principal Attack:

Strengths:

Weaknesses:

Time Travel!

It's time capsule time! Write a message to yourself: fill it with secret thoughts, a list of your favourite things and your hopes and dreams for the next year!

Then fold over the page and tape it shut.

See how it says 'DO NOT OPEN FOR ONE YEAR'? Do that.

Until next year!

TURN THE PAGE TO WRITE YOUR NOTES

DO NOT OPEN FOR ONE YEAR!

fold here

TIME CAPSULE MESSAGE to Your Future Self: ________________

____

____

Favourite things right now: ________________________

____

____

Things you hate right now: ________________________

____

____

Hopes and dreams for next year: ____________________

____

____

____

YOUR OWN
Last Kids on Earth Book!

Now it's your turn. Write your own original story about Jack, June, Quint and Dirk. Or write about the bad guys! Or write about Rover!

Feeling stuck? Here are a few ideas. . .

Figure out how the heroes will escape a horde of zombies, working together, combining their unique strengths to succeed. Or . . .

June and a friendly monster imagine their own amusement park. One that both monsters and humans can enjoy.

Create a new Feat of Apocalyptic Success and send the characters after it!

Write all about what Evie and Thrull would do if they hung out together for a day!

Max has a sister who is eight years younger than him. She's rad.

Now just write whatever you want!

Max Brallier's favourite book of all time is *Bart Simpson's Guide to Life*.

Take a rest! You've earned it!

© Ruby Brallier

MAX BRALLIER!

(maxbrallier.com) is the *New York Times* bestselling author of more than thirty books and games, including the Last Kids on Earth series. He writes both children's books and adult books, including the Galactic Hot Dogs series and the pick-your-own-path adventure *Can YOU Survive the Zombie Apocalypse?* He has written books for properties including *Adventure Time, Regular Show, Steven Universe, Uncle Grandpa* and *Poptropica*.

Under the pen name Jack Chabert, he is the creator and author of the Eerie Elementary series for Scholastic Books as well as the author of the *New York Times* bestelling graphic novel *Poptropica: Book 1: Mystery of the Map*. Previously, he worked in the marketing department at St. Martin's Press. Max lives in New York with his wife, Alyse, who is way too good for him. His daughter, Lila, is simply the best.

Follow Max on Twitter @MaxBrallier.

The author building his own tree house as a kiddo.

DOUGLAS HOLGATE!

(skullduggery.com.au) has been a freelance comic book artist and illustrator based in Melbourne, Australia, for more than ten years. He's illustrated books for publishers such as HarperCollins, Penguin Random House, Hachette and Simon & Schuster, including the Planet Tad series, Cheesie Mack, Case File 13 and *Zoo Sleepover*.

Douglas has illustrated comics for Image, Dynamite, Abrams, and Penguin Random House. He's currently working on the self-published series Maralinga, which received grant funding from the Australian Society of Authors and the Victorian Council for the Arts, as well as the all-ages graphic novel *Clem Hetherington and the Ironwood Race*, published by Scholastic Graphix, both co-created with writer Jen Breach.

Follow Douglas on Twitter @douglasbot.